SOMEWHERE IN THE CITY

J. B. Frank

ILLUSTRATED BY
Yu Leng

To the memory of my dad and to Annie,
my niece, who inspired me.
—JBF

Published by Familius LLC, www.familius.com
1254 Commerce Way, Sanger, CA 93657

Familius books are available at special discounts for bulk purchases, whether for sales promotions or for family or corporate use. For more information, contact Familius Sales at 559-876-2170 or email orders@familius.com.

Library of Congress Control Number: 2020950035

ISBN 9781641702607
eISBN 9781641704915
KF 9781641705158
FE 9781641705356

Printed in China

Edited by Maggie Wickes
Cover and book design by Brooke Jorden

10 9 8 7 6 5 4 3 2 1

First Edition

Somewhere in the city,
Lucy's just not ready to go to bed.
She opens her bedroom window and
lets in the bustle of the street below.

Stores are closing.
A scruffy dog sniffs an empty pail.
"Daddy's coming home," she calls to the dog.

WOOF-
WOOF!
barks the dog.

Somewhere in the city,
Daddy hurries through his work.
He grabs his jacket.
He waves to his coworkers.

"I've got to get home," he says as he pushes through the revolving door.

SWISH, SWISH spins the door.

Somewhere in the city,
Lucy watches as a baker pours
milk into a large bowl.

She takes a wooden spoon and stirs.
Flour spills, creating a smoky cloud around her.

MIX, MIX

moves the baker.

Somewhere in the city,
Daddy rushes down a busy street.
A musician plays a lullaby to the
people passing by.

Friends wave and invite Daddy to stop—
just for a minute or two?
"My little one needs me to tuck her in!"
he explains and hurries on.

"GOOD NIGHT,
GOOD NIGHT!"

call the friends.

Somewhere in the city,
Lucy puts on her pajamas and yawns.

From her window, she sees a woman waiting at the bus stop. The woman holds a grocery bag. She yawns too.

"Where are you, Daddy?"
Lucy asks as she watches
the bus drive up.

HISS-HISS

brakes the bus.

Somewhere in the city,
Daddy passes a construction site.
The crane rumbles to a halt,
and a bulldozer blocks the way.

Back and forth the bulldozer
moves until it fits just right.

Daddy checks his watch.
They call, "All clear!"

THUMP, THUMP

hurry his feet.

Somewhere in the city,
Lucy brushes her teeth.
She washes her face and makes funny faces in the mirror.

She swirls the soapy water with her finger, making letters.

GURGLE, GURGLE swirls the water.

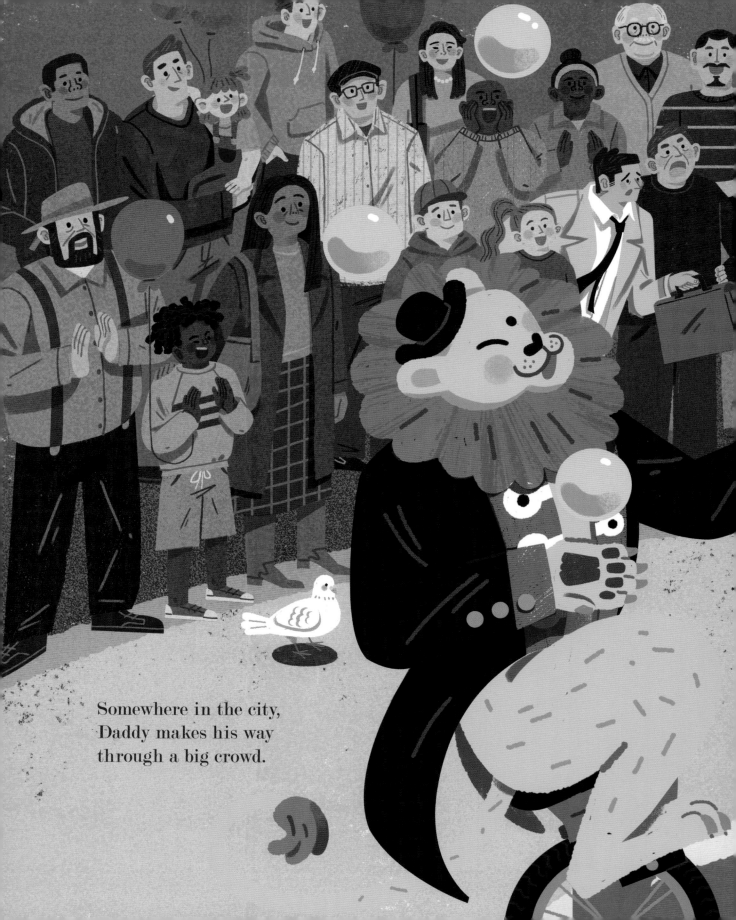

Somewhere in the city,
Daddy makes his way
through a big crowd.

A man juggles six balls in the air.
A woman gasps as the juggler throws
them higher and higher.

My Lucy would love this,
Daddy thinks, moving past.

"WOW, WOW!"

cheers the crowd.

Somewhere in the city,
Mommy calls. "Time for bed, my little sleepyhead."
But Lucy can't sleep without hearing that special something.

She watches a street sweeper removing all the dirt from the day.

Where does all that dirt go? Lucy wonders.

SH-H-H, SH-H-H
wipe the brushes.

Somewhere in the city,
Daddy bounces back and
forth on the train.
The train carries him
past neon lights that blink

COME ON IN!

He passes tree-lined streets crowded with cars and people walking.

speeds the train.

Somewhere in the city,
Lucy slowly sways to the music
drifting up from the grocery store below.
A worker washes the floor.
He swishes the mop to the rhythm of a song.

"WISHING, WISHING" sings the voice.

Somewhere in the city,
A daddy hurries.
A child waits.

The stars twinkle. The moon rises full and bright.
A cat walks through the alley. A dog barks.
This way to home. To Lucy.

"DADDY, DADDY!" giggles Lucy.

Somewhere in the city,
Daddy reads Lucy a bedtime story.
Lucy snuggles close.

Resting her head on his chest,
she hears that special something.

SIGH, SIGH

smiles Lucy.

Somewhere in the city.